SOLOMON THE LION

Written and illustrated by

Kristina Jones

Once there was a lion named

SOLOMON

SOLOMON was like most lions in *almost* every way ...

☑ Lions can **RUN** up to 80km/hour

☑ Lions have the loudest **ROAR** of any big cat

X Lions **SLEEP** 16 hours a day

... except for the sleeping part.

No matter how hard he tried,

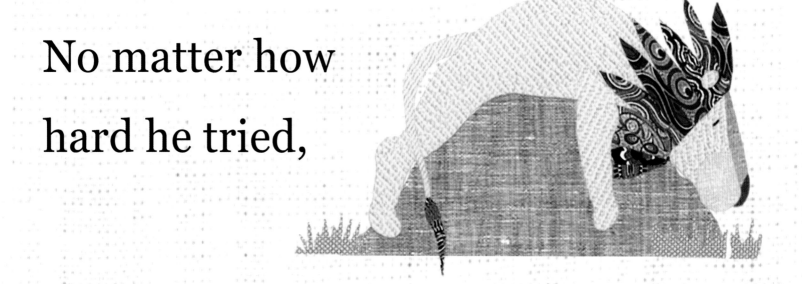

he just couldn't fall asleep.

He saw all the other animals sleeping

and wondered how they slept so peacefully.

He tried sleeping in a

NEST

like a

STORK,

in the
WATER

like a
HIPPO,

STANDING

like a **ZEBRA** ,

like a **SNAKE** ,

and even

UPSIDE
DOWN

like a
BAT

but poor **SOLOMON**

still couldn't

SLEEP

Feeling sad and tired,

SOLOMON sat down

to think.

Maybe it wasn't *where* you slept ...

maybe...

just maybe...

it was who you

KISSED GOODNIGHT.

Published in 2020 by Struik Children
an imprint of Penguin Random House South Africa (Pty) Ltd
Company Reg. No. 1953/000441/07
The Estuaries, 4 Oxbow Crescent, Century Avenue,
Century City 7441, Cape Town, South Africa
PO Box 1144, Cape Town 8000, South Africa
www.penguinrandomhouse.co.za

Publisher: Beverley Dodd
Managing editor: Cecilia Barfield
Editor: Gill Gordon
Designer: Jade Ludski

Printed and bound in China by RR Donnelley Asia Printing
Solutions Ltd

ISBN 978-1-43231-043-1